SARAH

Marmaduke the Magic Cat

Colin West

h
*Hodder
Children's
Books*

A division of Hodder Headline plc

I often visit my grandma who lives
the other side of town. I like to
help her out.

One day we were returning from
the supermarket with the shopping.
We were passing the library when
we noticed a scruffy black cat
ahead of us.

Instead of scampering away as we approached, the cat came right up and started rubbing against Grandma's leg, purring happily.

We couldn't resist stroking him. And what a funny cat he was.

His coat was bare in many places and his left ear was mauled as though he'd been in one scrap too many. He was wearing a bright tartan collar, and had a crooked little mouth which seemed to be curving into a smile.

The cat really loved being stroked, and soon Grandma bent down and started tickling him under the chin.

Grandma was enjoying it too. But after a while, she straightened up and said we should be making our way home.

But the cat had other ideas. As we
walked along, the cat followed.
Grandma spoke to him firmly.

You're a very
friendly cat, but
we must be on
our way, so
goodbye now!

Grandma gave the cat one last pat on
the head and started walking again.

But the funny cat followed us all the
way home to Grandma's front gate.

Then something very strange
happened. The gate opened
all by itself.

"It must have been a gust of wind,"
said Grandma, looking rather
puzzled. She turned her door key and
we went inside.

As we put down the shopping bags,
we quite forgot about the funny cat.
But then Grandma went to shut the
door, and there on the mat was the
mischievous moggy!

"He's very friendly!" I said.

"Can we give him some cream?"

Alright, but then we must say goodbye to him.

We all went in the kitchen. Grandma poured some cream into a saucer, and the cat quickly lapped it up.

Then another amazing thing happened. The saucer floated from the floor and hovered in mid-air, doing a sort of aerobatic dance.

The saucer landed gently by the
kitchen sink.
"What on earth's happening?" asked
Grandma as she pulled up a chair.

I scratched my head.
"What shall we do with him?"
I asked.

The cat was standing at our feet,
wearing a naughty grin. I noticed
a gold disc on his collar.
"There's an address here!" I said,
examining the disc.

Marmaduke
Cobblestone Cottage
Forest Road
Middlewick.

I read the address out loud and
Grandma turned pale.
"Cobblestone Cottage," she muttered.
"Now it's falling into place."

"What do you mean?" I asked.
Grandma took a deep breath.

Cobblestone Cottage is a spooky place. Everyone says the woman who lives there is a witch.

I couldn't believe that Grandma, a grown lady, could believe in witches.

But witches only exist in Fairy Tales!

"Come on," I said. "Let's take
Marmaduke back."
Grandma agreed it was the best
thing to do, all said and done.

She put the cat under her arm and
we left for Cobblestone Cottage.

Chapter Two

As we passed the traffic lights at the crossroads, the third really strange thing happened. The lights which were red, suddenly turned purple, then blue, and then pink!

Cars started hooting and drivers
shouting.

"Stop that mischief," Grandma said to

the cat in her arms.
Marmaduke winked an eye at me
and I couldn't help smiling back.

Past the shops, up the hill and by
the forest we reached Cobblestone
Cottage. It did look rather spooky.

We nervously walked up the path.
The front door had peeling paint
and an old brass knocker at the
centre. I gave it three loud raps.

After a while, we heard footsteps
from inside, and the heavy door
creaked open.

Standing there was a figure with
wild frizzy hair, big round glasses
and crazy, coloured clothes.
She didn't look like anyone's idea
of a witch.

"Marmaduke, darling!" she cried,
opening her arms.
The cat purred happily as she
cuddled him and tickled his chin.

We were soon joined by lots of other cats who came from all directions.

A Siamese, a Persian and a Tabby all
gathered round to greet Marmaduke.

"How kind of you to return him," said the multi-coloured lady.

Now, you must come inside – I was just about to put the kettle on.

Grandma and I loooked at each other and nodded rather apprehensively. We followed the woman inside.

Her home was full of cats.

There were cats on the sofa,
cats on the mantelpiece,
cats in the cupboards,
cats everywhere!

"My name's Muriel, by the way,"
said the lady. "Please make
yourselves at home."

Grandma and I perched on a settee
and Muriel poured three mugs of
herbal tea.
"Marmaduke obviously likes you," she
commented, as the cat snuggled up
beside Grandma.

We smiled politely and sipped our tea.
"They were all strays once, you
know," said Muriel proudly pointing
to the felines all around.

We nodded and she handed round
some carrot cake.

31

Then Grandma cleared her throat,
as though she were about to say
something important.

Pardon me, but
strange things seem
to happen when
Marmaduke's
around.

"Naughty Marmaduke, I'm afraid
some of my magic has rubbed
off on him!"

Grandma and I looked at each other, wide-eyed.

"Then you are a witch?" I asked.

"Yes, of course I am!" she laughed.

But not all witches are evil, you know. Most of us are good, and we like to help people out.

We both breathed a sigh of relief.

"Now," said Muriel, leaning forward.
"I wonder if I may ask you a favour?"
Grandma and I looked at each other
once more.

What is it?

Muriel pointed to the cat on
Grandma's lap.

Marmaduke has
clearly taken a shine
to you. How about
looking after
him for me?

Grandma was taken aback.
She lived álone and had often
thought about a pet for company.
But this mischievous magical cat?

Well, I'm not sure...

"I know he's found a good home,"
Muriel went on, "and he's an
independent cat who's perfectly
happy by himself."

But Grandma wasn't convinced.

I'm very fond of Marmaduke, but I'm not sure about all those magic tricks of his.

"Ahhh!" sighed Muriel. "That might
be a problem. You see, once a witch's
cat, always a witch's cat."
She thought for a while and then
jumped up excitedly.

Muriel waved her arms around and
lots of magic stars appeared.

After a magic spell, Muriel was
suddenly wearing a crash helmet
and sturdy boots. "Now let's get
round to your place!" she announced.

Grandma borrowed a spare crash helmet and we followed Muriel outside. She rummaged around in the shed for a tool box. Then she wheeled out an old motorcycle combination.

Grandma sat behind her, and I sat
with Marmaduke in the sidecar.

In a cloud of purple dust, we
roared off to Grandma's.

Chapter Three

At Grandma's front door, Muriel
got to work straightaway.
She waved her arms around
frantically and chanted a magic
spell: Kattaflapperus!

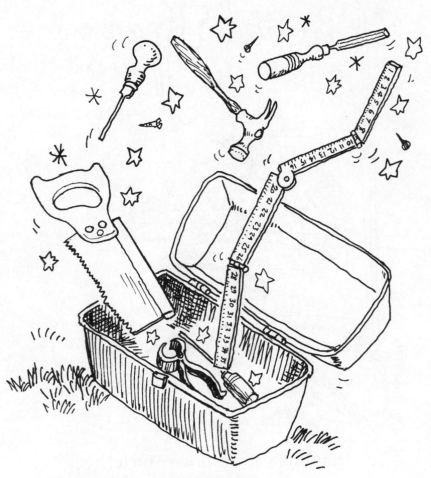

Once again, lots of magic stars
appeared. Then Muriel's tool box
came to life. The lid opened and
the tools started dancing around.

Then Muriel looked at the front door closely and said some more magic words.

Then the saw started sawing,

the hammer started hammering,

and the chisel started chiselling.

A neat little square hole appeared
in the door in next-to-no-time.

Before much longer, a flap on
hinges had been fitted.

Muriel explained things.

"Now this is a magic cat flap . . ."

Muriel coaxed Marmaduke to walk in the cat flap.

Then Muriel added: "And when
Marmaduke goes out, his mischief
and magic are restored!"

As Marmaduke walked out, some
pink and purple stars appeared as
he squeezed through the flap.

Marmaduke soon got up to his mischief. In the front garden, he made a flower pot dance round the lawn.

Then he made a concrete gnome do a double somersault.

A passer-by rubbed her eyes in
astonishment as the gnome landed
on the gate post.

49

Muriel and I chuckled to ourselves.
But Grandma still looked a bit
worried.

"Don't worry, Marmaduke will be as
good as gold when he's indoors,"
Muriel reassured her.

Then Muriel waved her arms around again and all the tools jumped back into the tool box.

We thanked Muriel as she put on
her crash helmet. She tickled
Marmaduke under the chin, said
goodbye and roared off on her
motorbike.

Chapter Four

Things went well for a while.
Grandma was happy not to be
living alone, and Marmaduke was
well-behaved around the house.

Of course, Marmaduke got up to
mischief when he went through
the magic cat flap: the letter box
just outside Grandma's house often
spoke in a voice like a dalek.

And the sparrows in Grandma's back
garden sometimes flew upside down
and looped the loop. But those things
were only to be expected.

However, after a while Grandma noticed that Marmaduke was using his mischievous magic indoors too.

I wondered what had gone wrong.
I tried to tell off Marmaduke, but
he didn't seem to understand.

You shouldn't get up to mischief indoors, Marmaduke.

"Maybe we should take him back
to Muriel's," Grandma suggested,
although I don't think she really
meant it.

Then I noticed there was a bottom
window open, and it suddenly
dawned on me: if Marmaduke
came through the window, his
magic wouldn't be erased.

So, from then on, Grandma only left
top windows open.

Since then, the Magic Cat Flap has
worked a treat. Grandma has the
perfect indoor companion . . .

But she can often be seen standing
at her window watching the
mayhem outside . . .

The lollipop lady down the street
sometimes bursts into song, and
the children dance round her
lollipop.

And sometimes the clock on
St. Marks, opposite, goes
backwards and strikes thirteen.

Life is never dull in Grandma's neighbourhood, and of course, when something magical happens, Marmaduke is never far away!

The End